CHUGGINGTON™

WILSON and the ICE CREAM FAIR

Adapted by Mara Conlon
Based on the story by Jimmy Hibbert

SCHOLASTIC INC.
New York Toronto London Auckland
Sydney Mexico City New Delhi Hong Kong

ISBN 978-0-545-26631-4

© Ludorum plc 2011. Chuggington® is a registered trademark of Ludorum plc.
All rights reserved. Published by Scholastic Inc.
SCHOLASTIC and associated logos are trademarks and/or registered
trademarks of Scholastic Inc.
12 11 10 9 8 7 6 5 4   11 12 13 14 15/0

Printed in the U.S.A.   40
First printing, January 2011

Here comes Wilson.

"Choo! Choo!"

"I have a job for you," says Vee.
"The ice cream fair is today. Your job is
to take the ice cream to Farmer Felix."

"perfecto!"

says Wilson.

Wilson goes to get the ice cream.
"Load up!" he says.
The ice cream cars are heavy.
Wilson has to take one car at a time.

Wilson takes the first car to the fair.

Then he goes back to get more.

Here comes Frostini!
Wilson has to take more ice cream.
But he wants to see where the ice cream is made!

"Hi, Wilson!" says Frostini. "What brings you to the ice cream factory?"

"TOOT! TOOT!"

"I'm picking up ice cream! Will you show me where the ice cream is made?" Wilson asks.

"sure!" says Frostini.

Frostini takes Wilson inside.

He tells Wilson about making ice cream.

The chuggers go into the freezer room.
Frostini shows Wilson the flavors.

"Brrr! My wheels are cold!" says Wilson.

Farmer Felix is waiting at the fair.

Where is Wilson with the ice cream?

Wilson is late!

He lost track of time.

So he tries to pull all the cars at once.
But they are too heavy.
He can't do it alone!
Wilson needs Frostini's help!

Frostini is busy making ice cream.

"Ice cream! Ice cream!
It's cold. It's yummy.
Feels good in your tummy!"
says Frostini.

"Frostini, will you help me pull
the ice cream cars?" asks Wilson.
"But of course," says Frostini.

The two trains take all the ice cream cars together.

Wilson and Frostini arrive at
the Fair.
"We have all the ice cream!"
says Wilson.

"There is something even better than ice cream!" Wilson adds.

"What could be better?" asks Frostini.

"Good friends!"

says Wilson.